Samad in the Desert

SAMAD IN THE DESERT

Mohammed Umar

Illustrated by
Soukaina Lalla Greene

Salaam Publishing
London

First published in Great Britain 2016
Salaam Publishing
London
Salaampublishing@gmail.com
www.salaampublishing.com

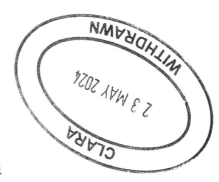

For Salim, Karim & Nafisa
M. U.

For Kevin Lyons
S.L.G.

Our heartfelt appreciation to
Cecilia Greene

Special thanks to
Samad, Fajr, Safia, Asghar, Sami, Lailuma & Irfan Ullah

Once upon a time there was a boy and his name was Samad. Samad's dream was to spend a whole day in the desert, meet the animals and swim in the oasis. After the animals met and heard about Samad's dream, they agreed to make it come true.

One cloudless morning Samad started his adventure into the desert.

First Samad saw an eagle that flew over him. Soon the bird sang for him.

Welcome to the desert
Where the air is still and warm
And water is scarce but sand is plenty
Where it's hard to play hide and seek
And humans are few and kind

And then Samad met three gazelles.

"So this is what a desert gazelle looks like," Samad said.

"So this is what Samad looks like," one gazelle said looking at Samad.

"Surprise," Samad heard from behind a rock. A desert fox emerged, excited.

"Why are you so excited?" Samad asked.

"I only come out at night, but today I came out in the daytime to meet you'"

"What is going on here?" Samad screamed. "Where is its head?"

"In the sand," an ostrich answered.

"Head in the sand?"

"Yes, ostriches can bury their heads in the sand."

"Catch me if you can," the ostrich said and started running. "Running on sand is fun. Whoever gets to the oasis first wins."

Samad accepted the challenge and ran ahead of the ostrich.

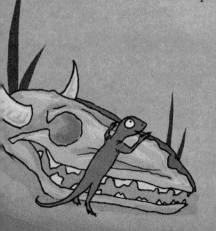

"I didn't expect to see a tortoise in the desert," Samad said.

"There are a few of us."

"How am I going to cross this dune to the oasis?"

"Don't worry, I'll carry you across," joked the tortoise.

"Hey Samad, I'll take you across the dunes to the oasis," a camel said. "But before that let's seek shelter because I can see a sandstorm coming."

"What! A sandstorm?" Samad exclaimed.

"Yes, a big sandstorm is approaching."

"Oh my God, this is scary," Samad said. "There's sand everywhere."

"That's life in the desert. Just be patient, it'll pass," said the fox.

After the storm had passed, the fox said. "I can smell rain in the air."

Soon it began to rain.

"How lucky we are to have a few drops of rain in one year," the camel said as they ran around in the rain.

After the rain, Samad and his companions continued their journey into the desert.

"I can see water in the distance."

"There's no water there. In the desert you see things that are not there. It's called mirage."

"I'm thirsty what about you?" Samad asked the camel.

"I'm not. I can go for two months without water."

"Look! There's an oasis down there," the camel said.

On the way to the oasis Samad stopped and admired a desert plant.

"Where does the water come from?" Samad asked.

"It comes from underground rivers," a frog replied.

"You mean there is water under the sand?"

"Yes."

"Wow," Samad said as he dived into the water.
"I'm so happy because my second dream has come true."

And then after sunset a group of bats flew past Samad whistling, "Good night Samad."

"Look, a star is falling!" Samad said later.

"No Samad! It's not falling. It's a shooting star," the fox explained.

Lightning Source UK Ltd.
Milton Keynes UK
UKOW07f1321280617
304248UK00001B/3/P